CW01207105

Hungry Kenneth

Written by Daniel Heath
Illustrated by Georgia Thomas

For my beautiful boys, Iago and Idris
Love Mum

In remembrance of Little Nanny, we miss you everyday

It was a sunny day, so Kenneth decided to go for a slither outside. He liked to feel the warm ground on his belly.

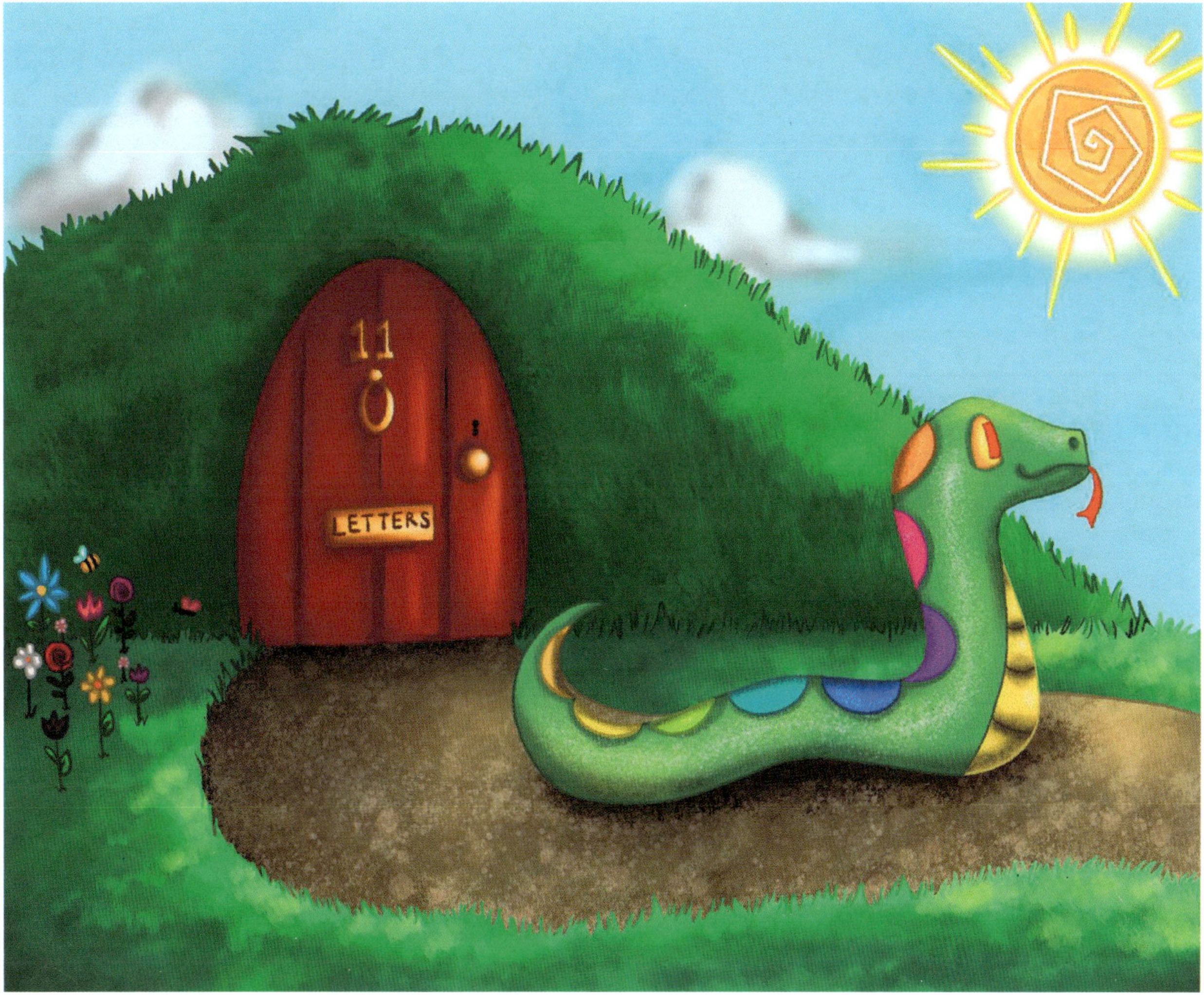
11
LETTERS

Once Kenneth got outside he started to feel a little peckish. He'd forgotten to have dinner last night because he had been watching a TV show about boats.

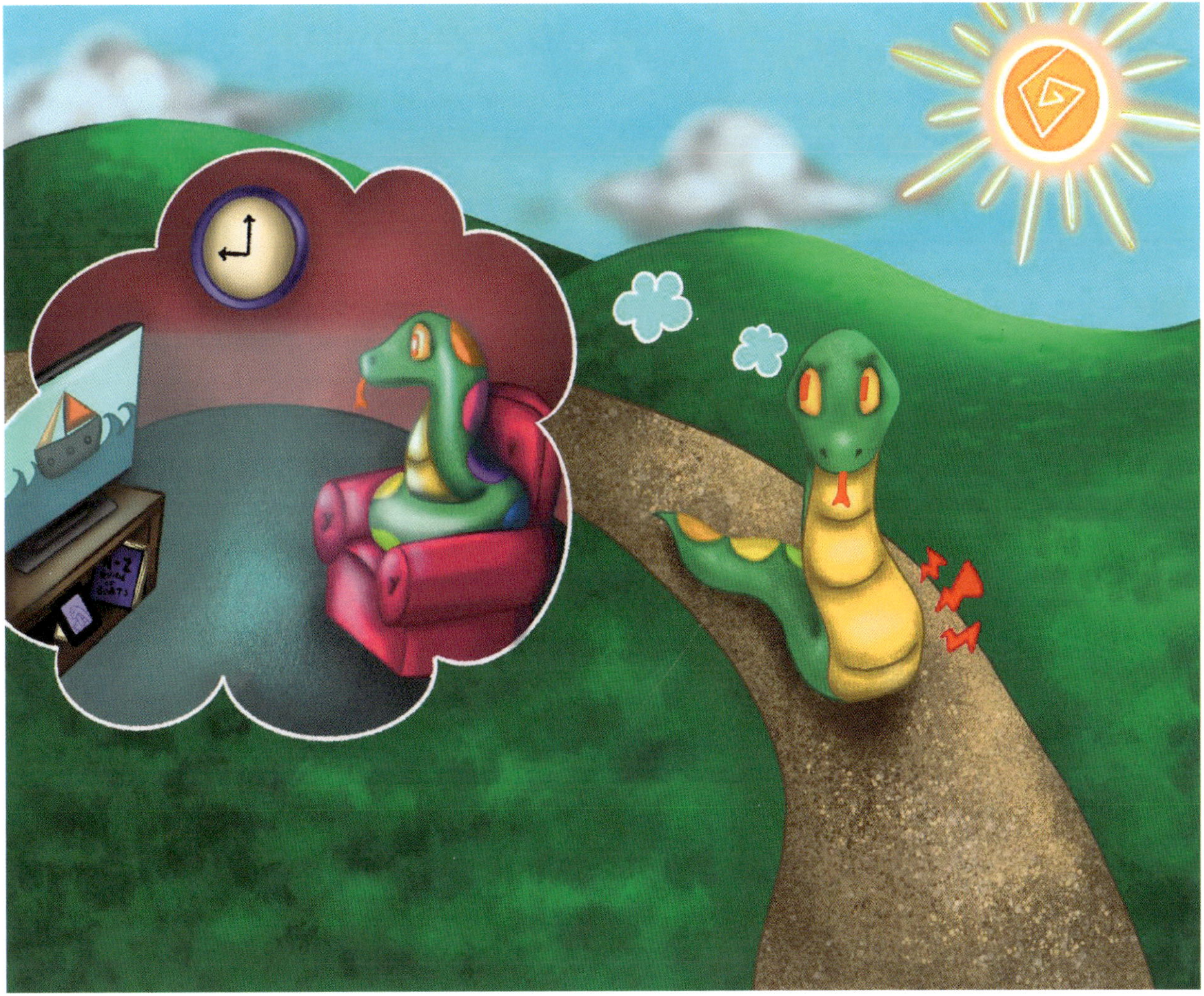

Now that Kenneth was outside he thought he'd try to find some of his friends, so he started by slithering into the field to see Julian. Julian was playing football.

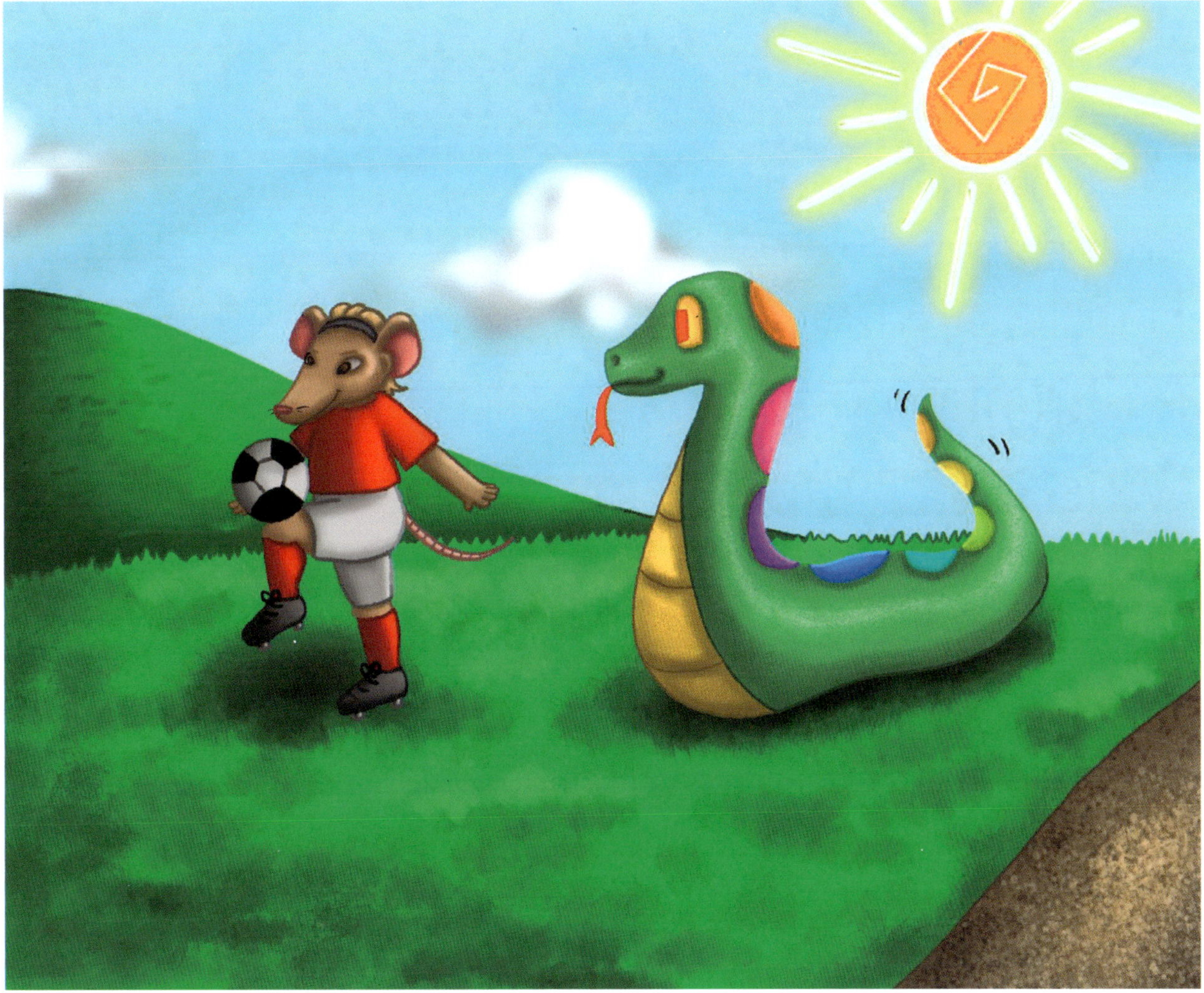

"Hi Julian, what are you up to?" said Kenneth. "I'm playing football" said Julian, "I like it when I kick the ball in the goal and put my hands in the air"

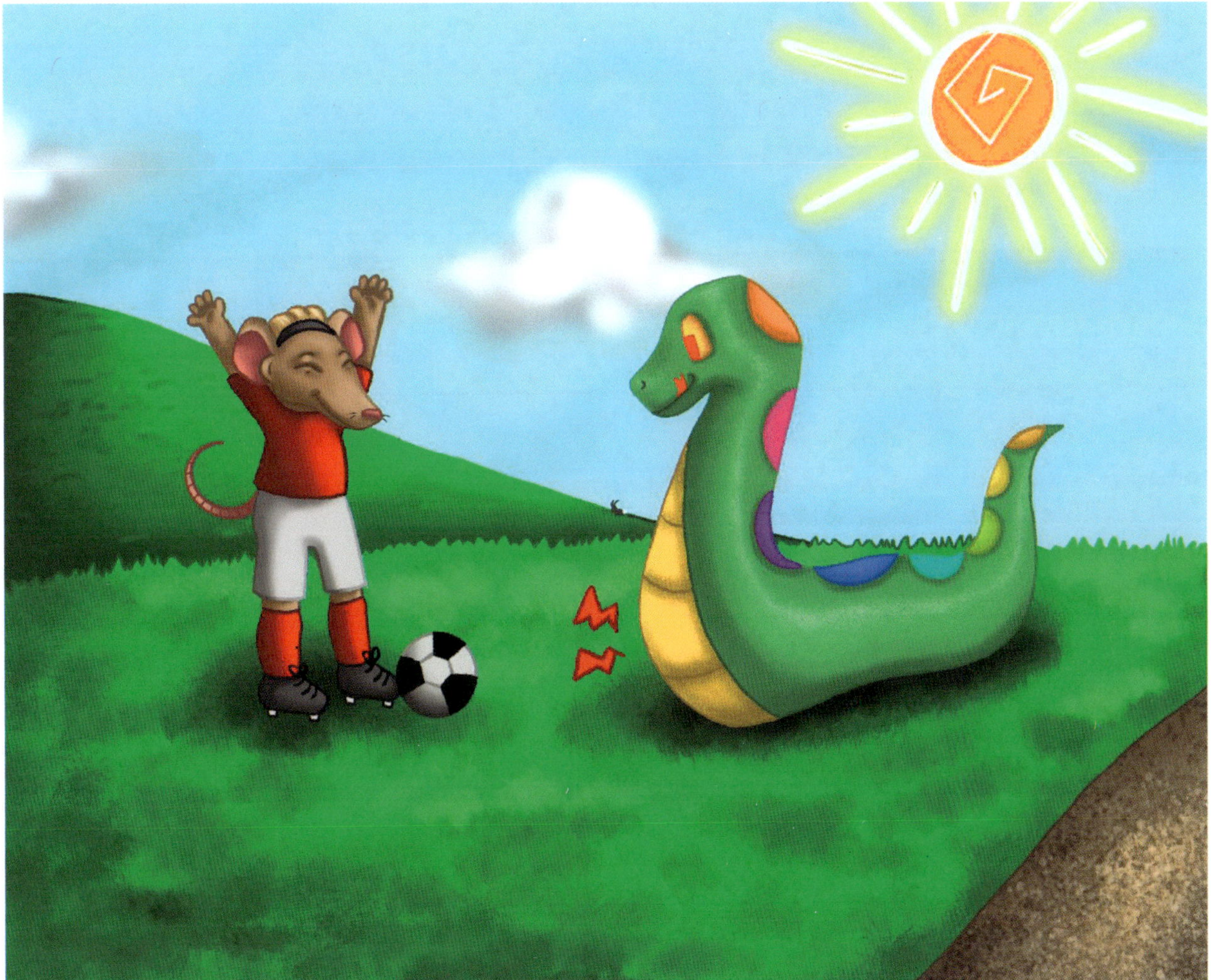

"Wait a minute" said Julian, "I can't find my ball…..have you seen it?"
"No" said Kenneth, "I can't remember seeing it to be honest"

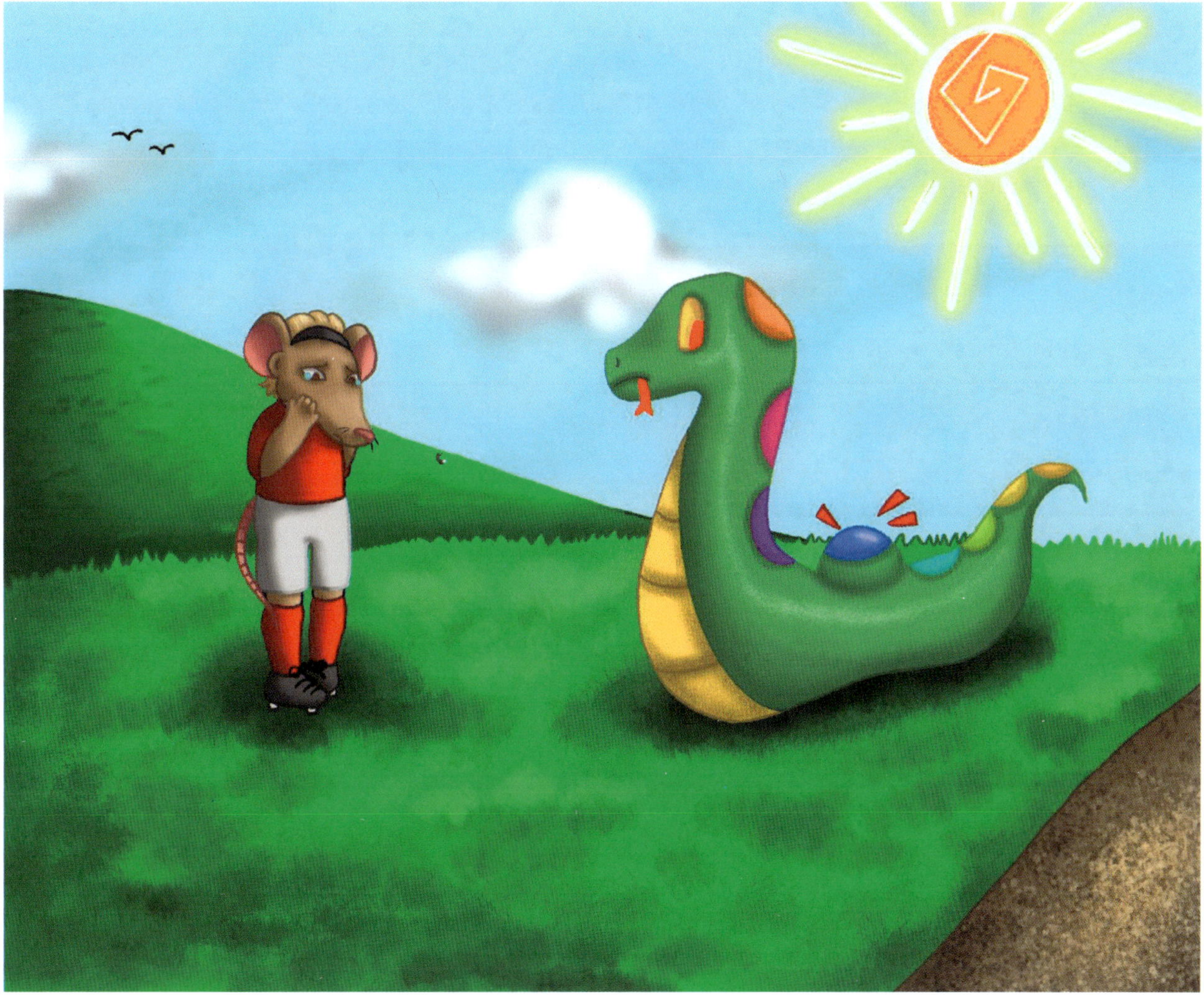

Kenneth slithered into the forest to see Susan. Susan was camping and frying some bacon.

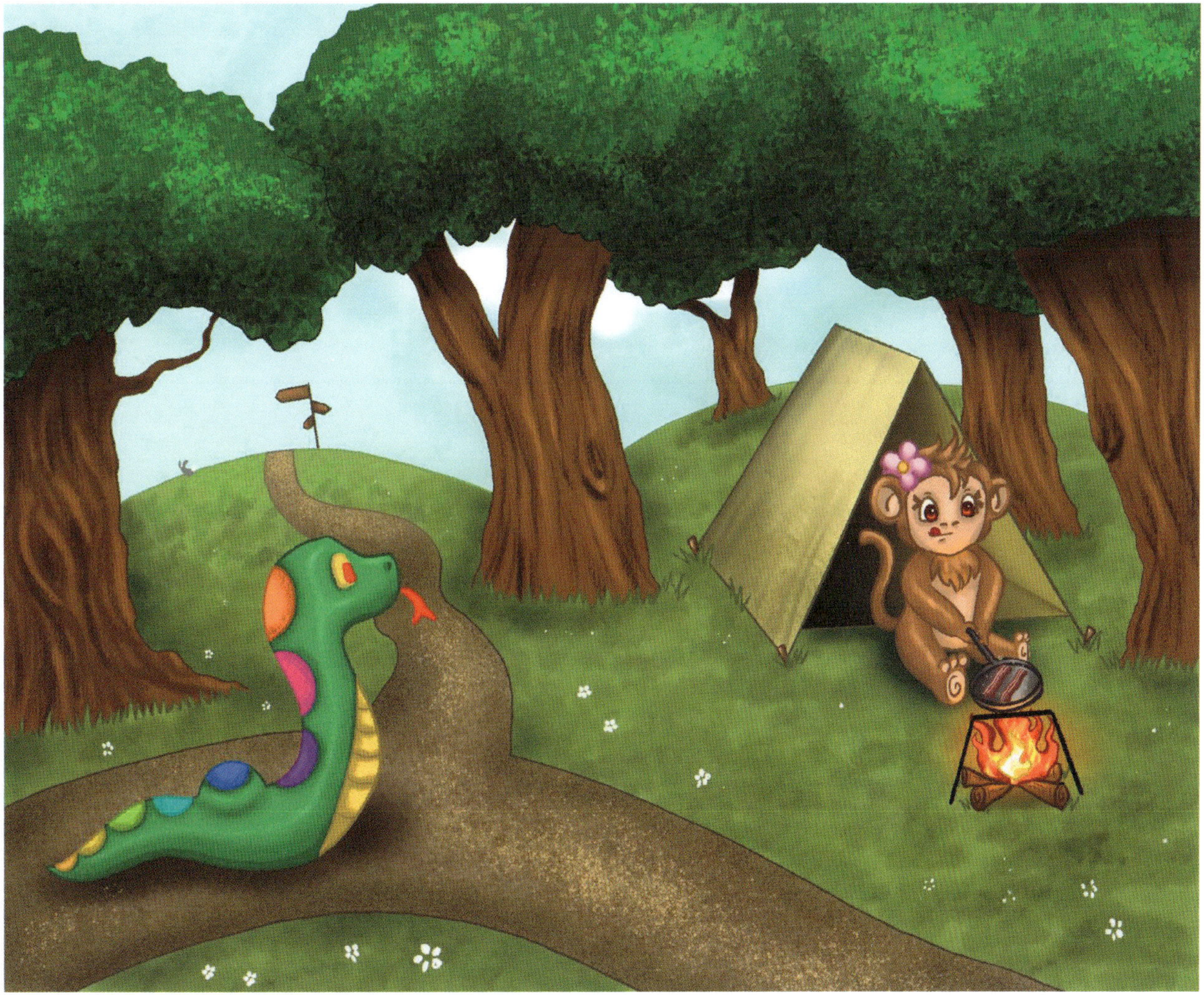

"Hi Susan, are you having fun?" said Kenneth. "Yes thank you" said Susan, "I love bacon so much, especially when it sizzles"

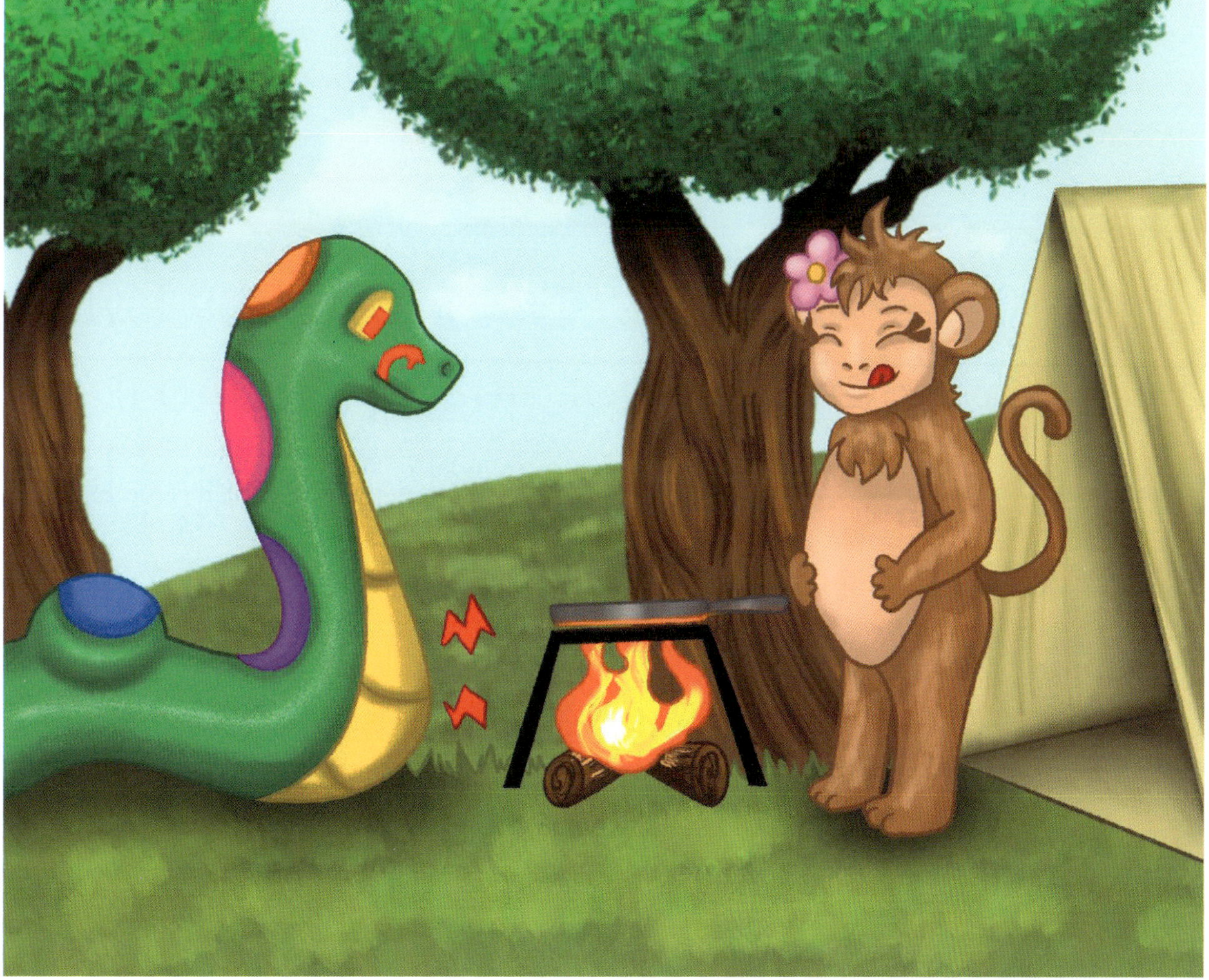

"Hold on" said Susan, "I can't find my frying pan.....I wonder what's happened to it"
"I have no idea" said Kenneth, "are you sure you had one?"

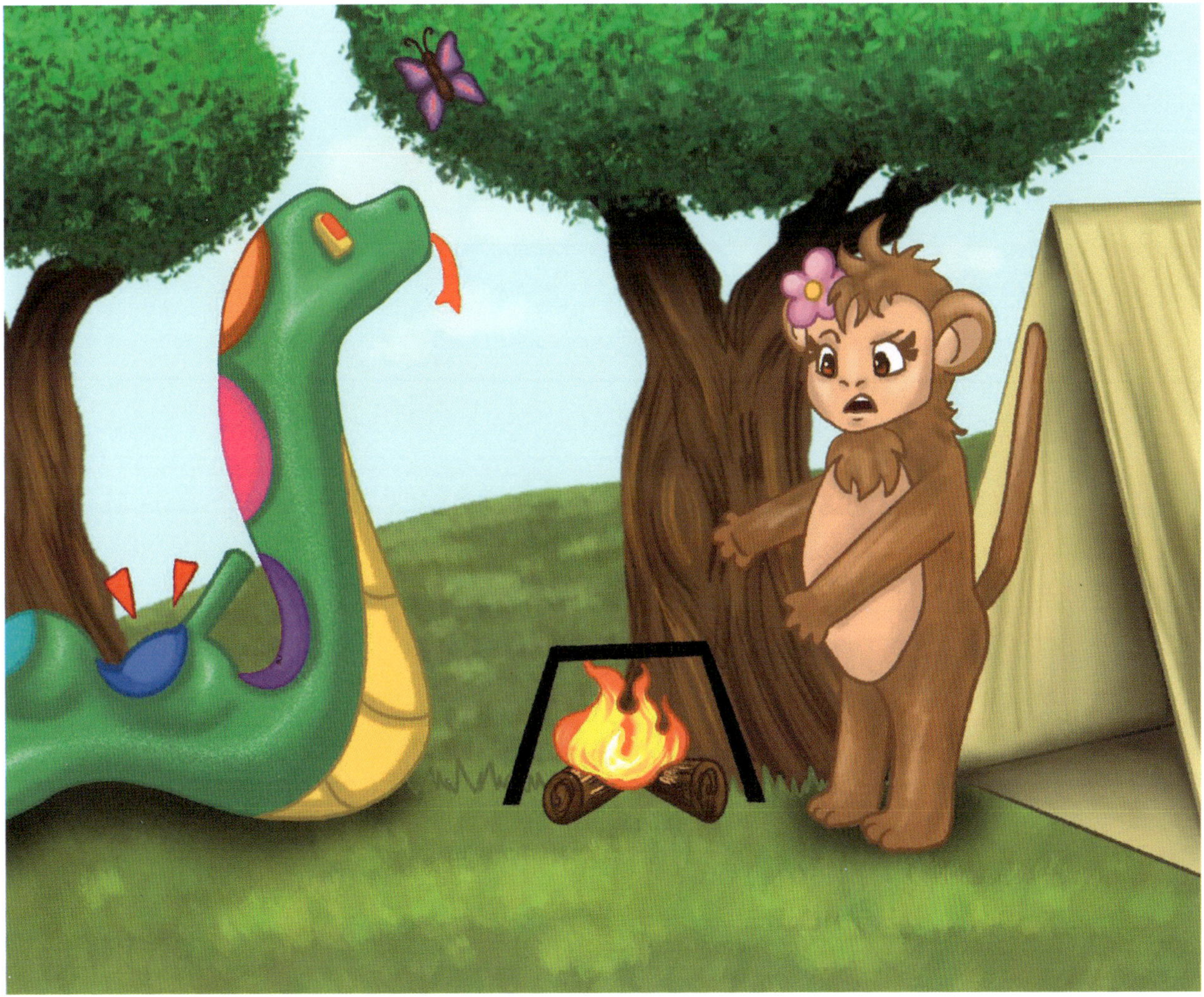

Kenneth slithered down towards the river to see Jean-Pierre. Jean-Pierre was fishing.

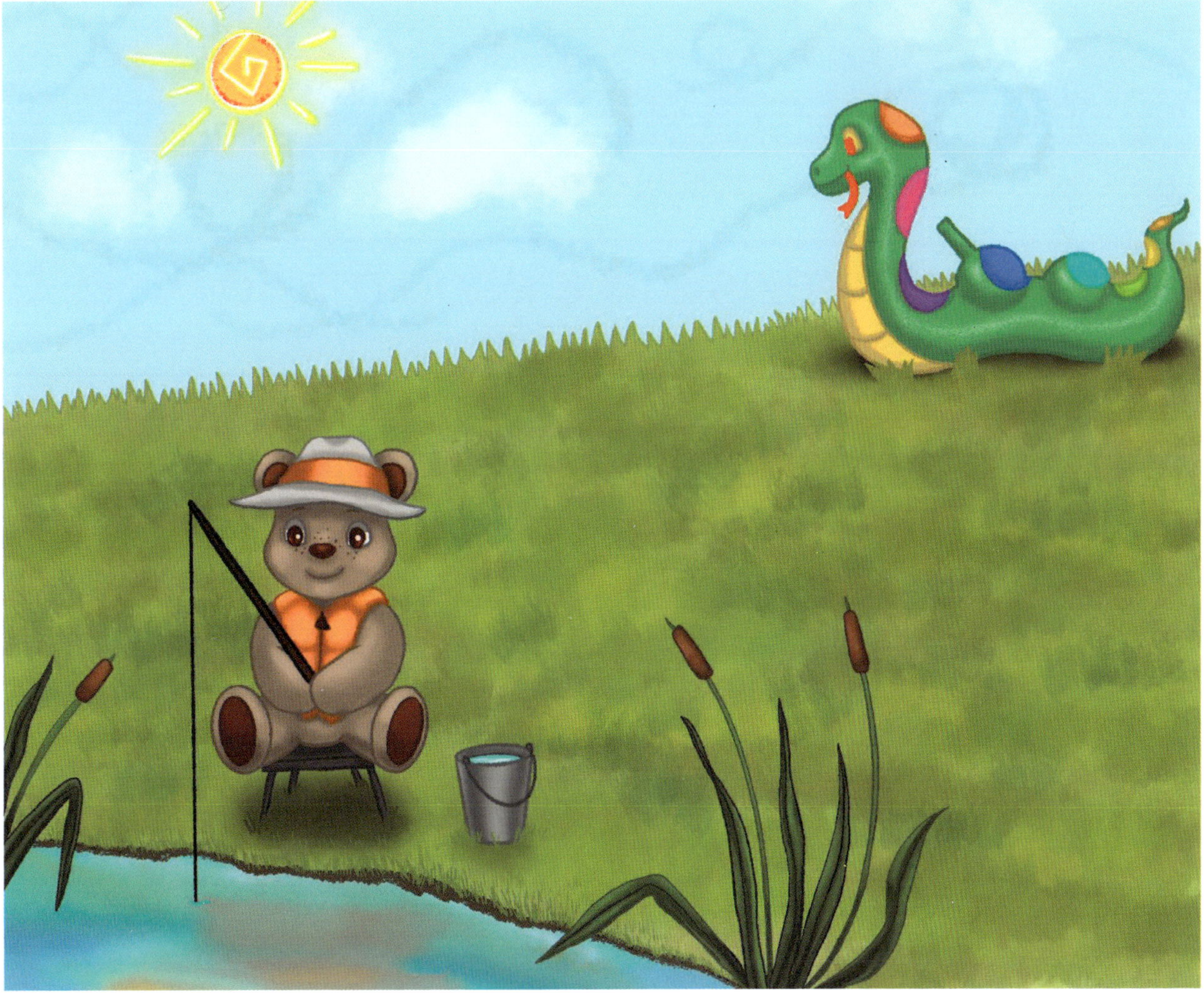

"Hi Jean-Pierre, is this a good day for you?" said Kenneth.
"It really is" said Jean-Pierre, "I like catching fish, but I also like plopping them back into the water and watching them swim fast"

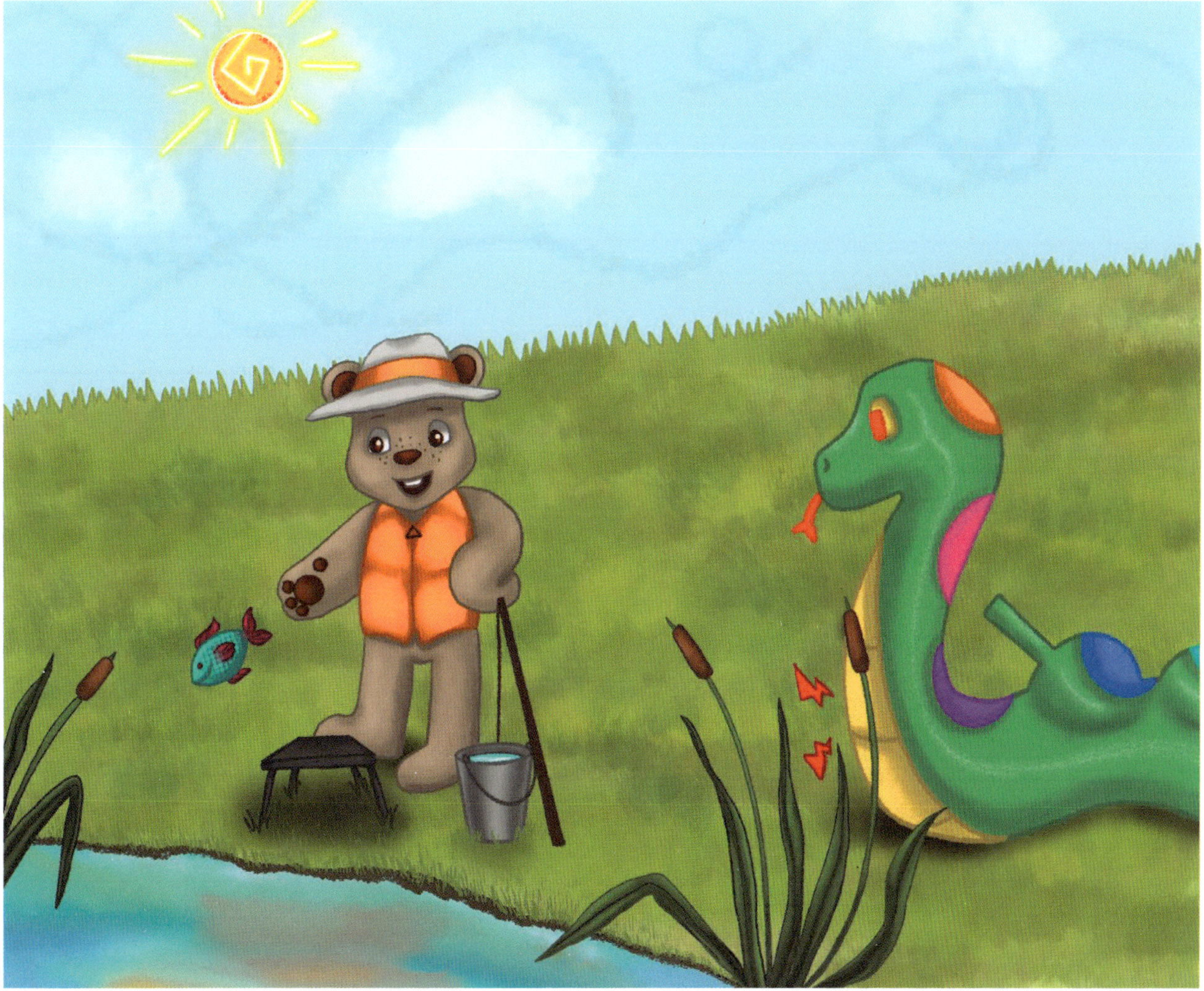

"Oh crumbs" said Jean-Pierre, "has anyone seen my fishing rod?"
"Not me" said Kenneth, "maybe you dropped it in the river and it floated away, like a leaf"

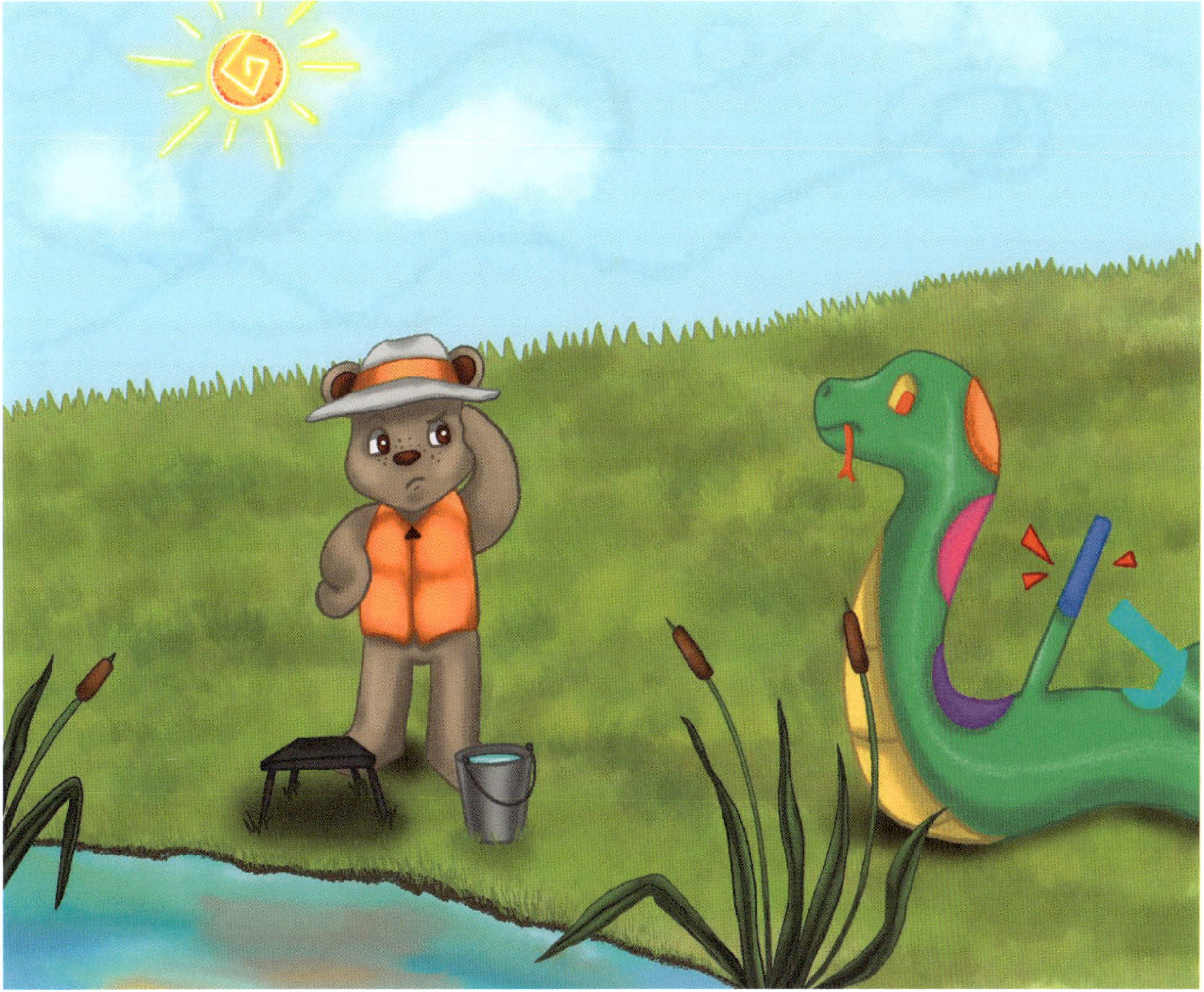

Kenneth slithered to the nearby sports club to see Liam. Liam was playing cricket.

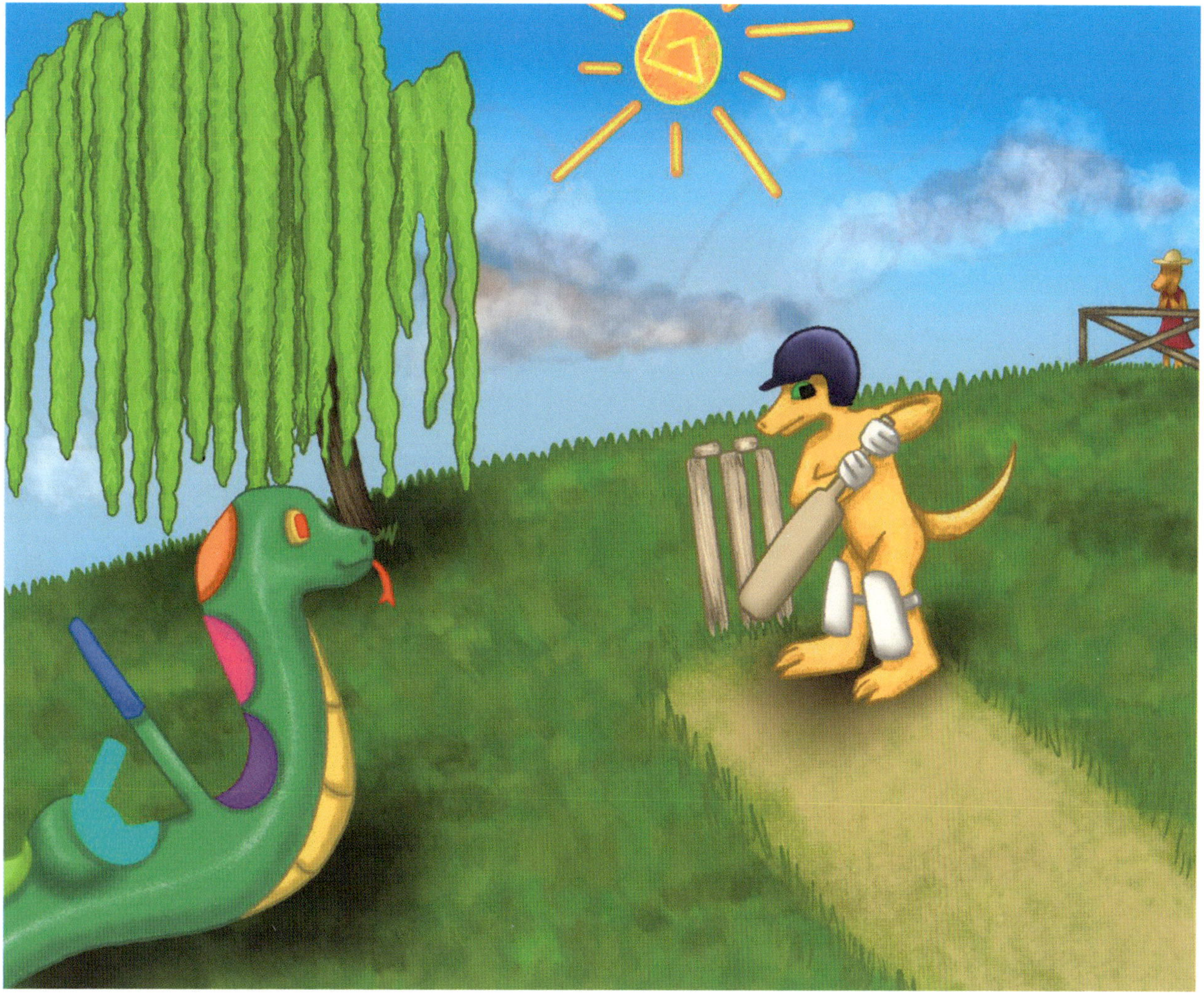

"Are you winning at cricket Liam?" asked Kenneth.
"I just hit a 6 and my Mum saw me do it" said Liam.

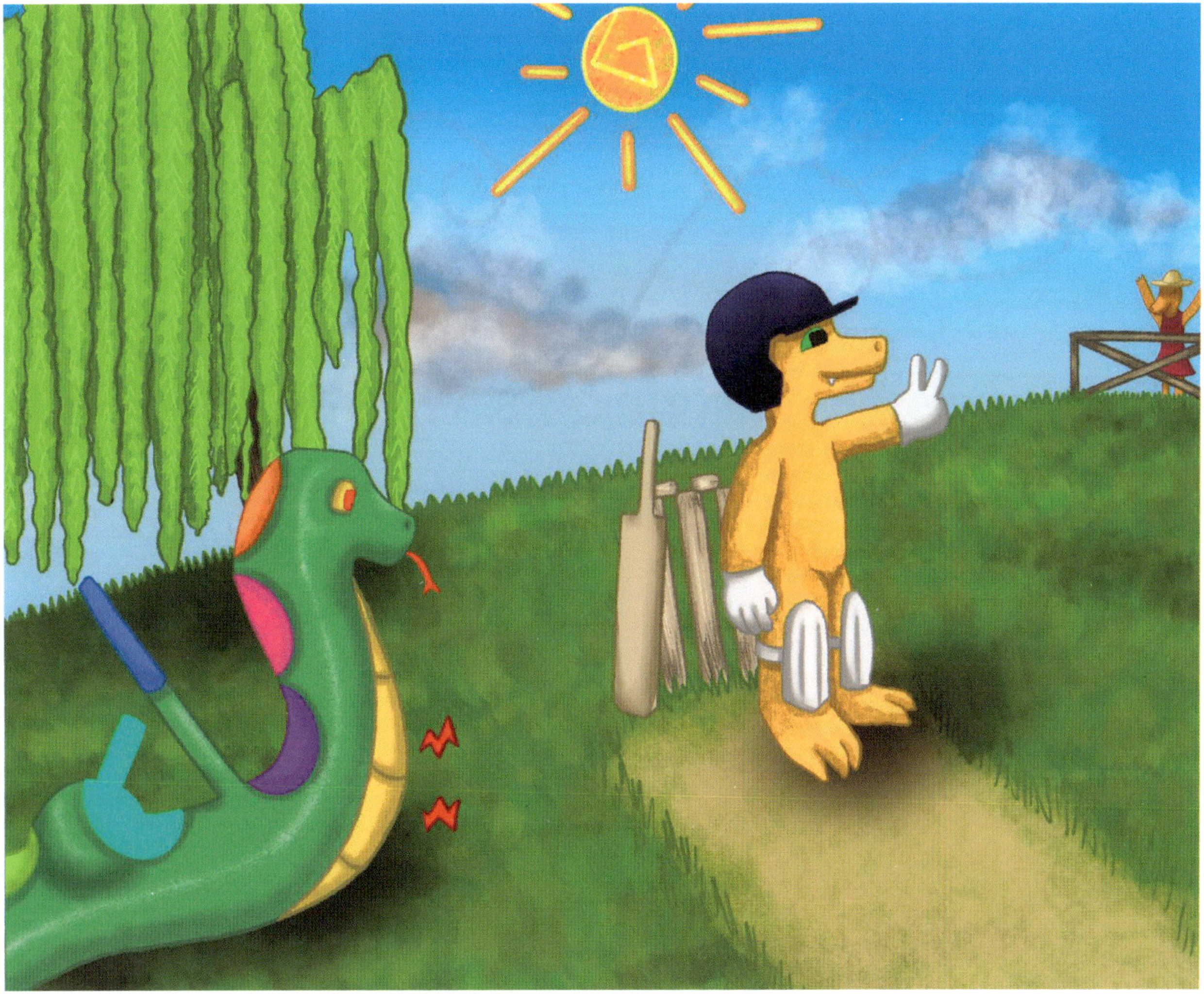

"Oh no no no" said Liam, "somebody has stolen my cricket bat I think"
"That's a nuisance" said Kenneth, "has your Mum got a spare?"

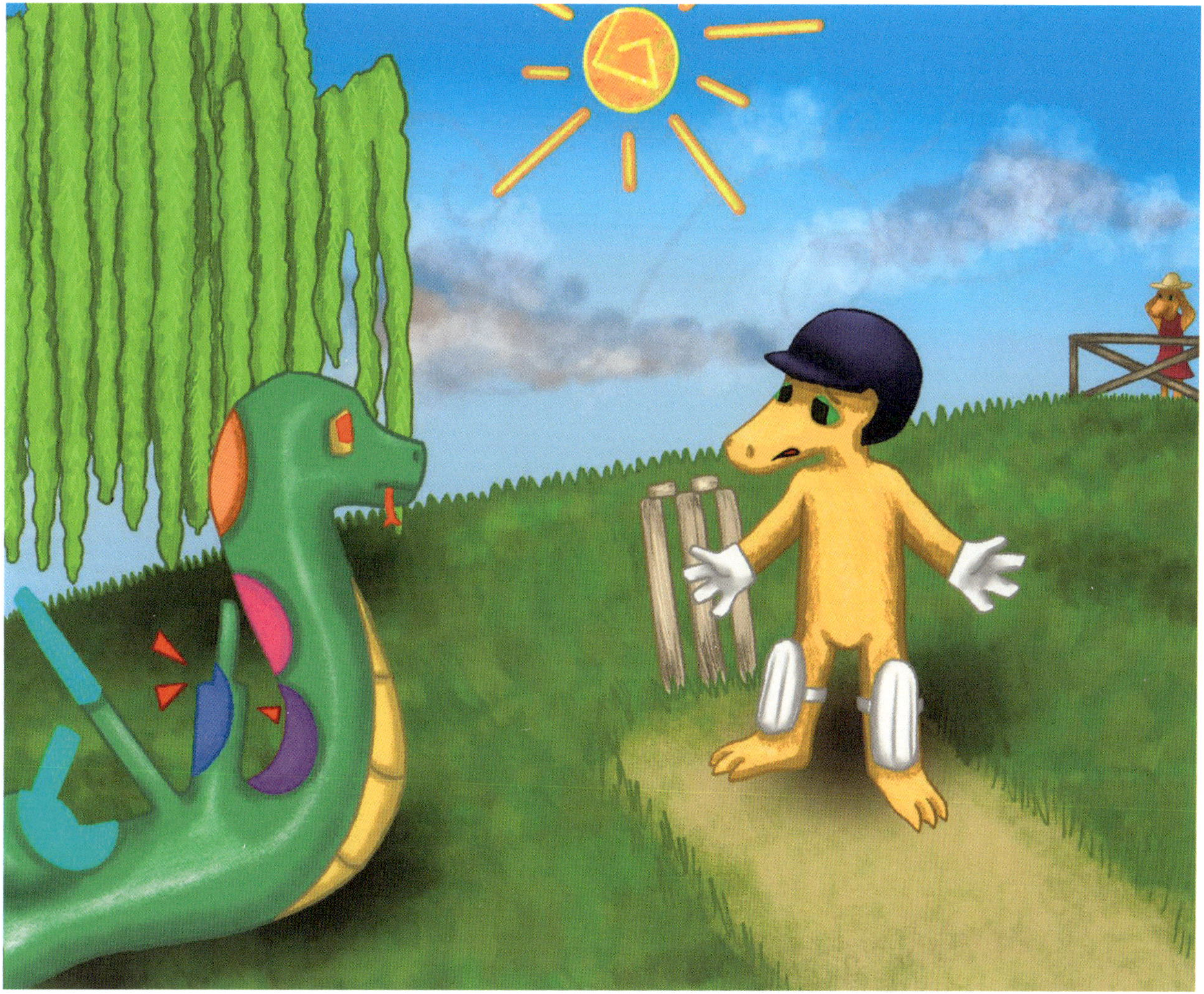

Kenneth slithered off away from his friends and lay on a bench, feeling sad and a bit ill. Melvin saw him and came over to say hello.

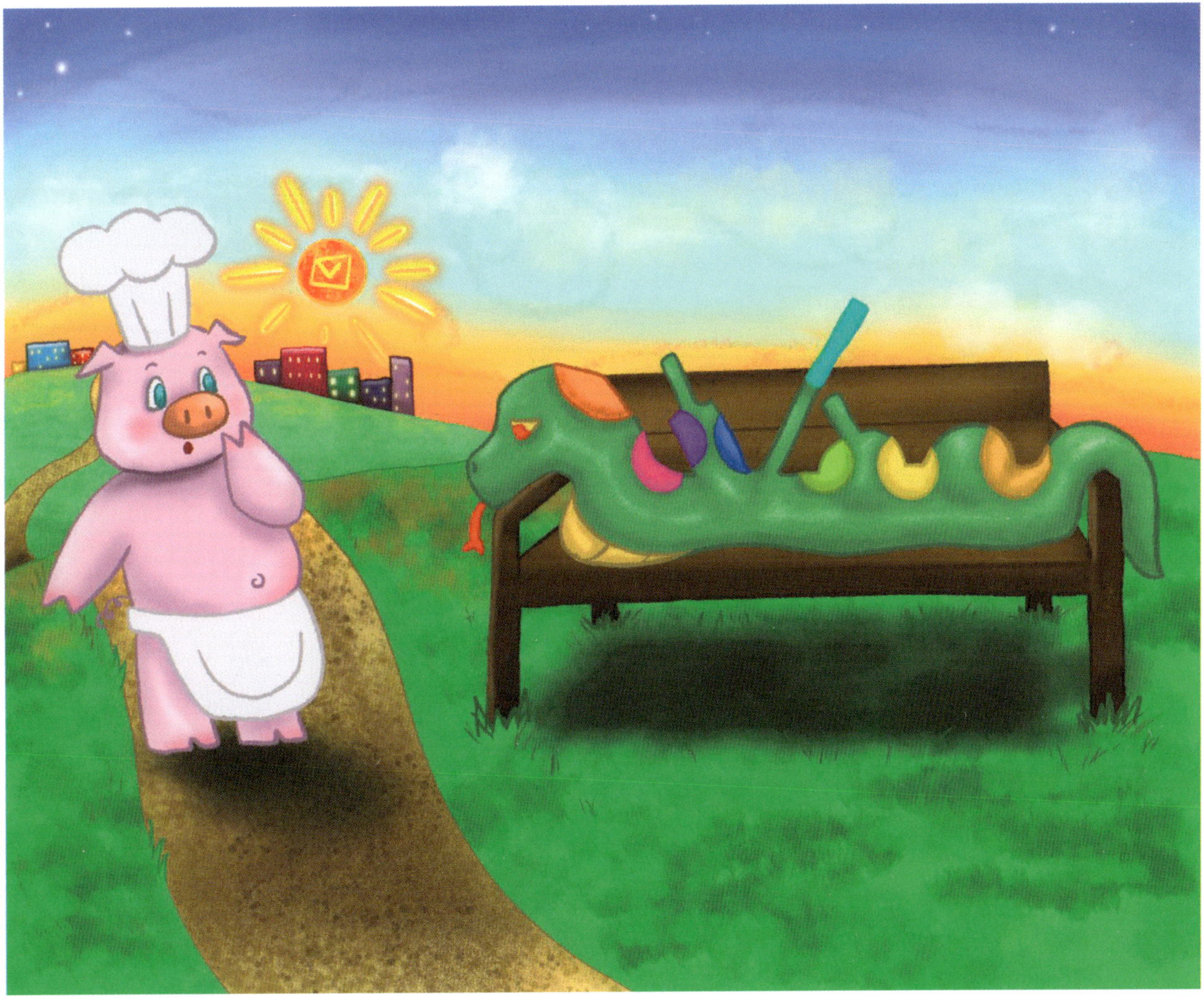

"Are you okay Kenneth?" said Melvin, "you seem a bit down in the dumps and a bit glum"

"My friends don't want me around because I keep eating all their stuff" said Kenneth, "they made me slither away from them and their fun activities"

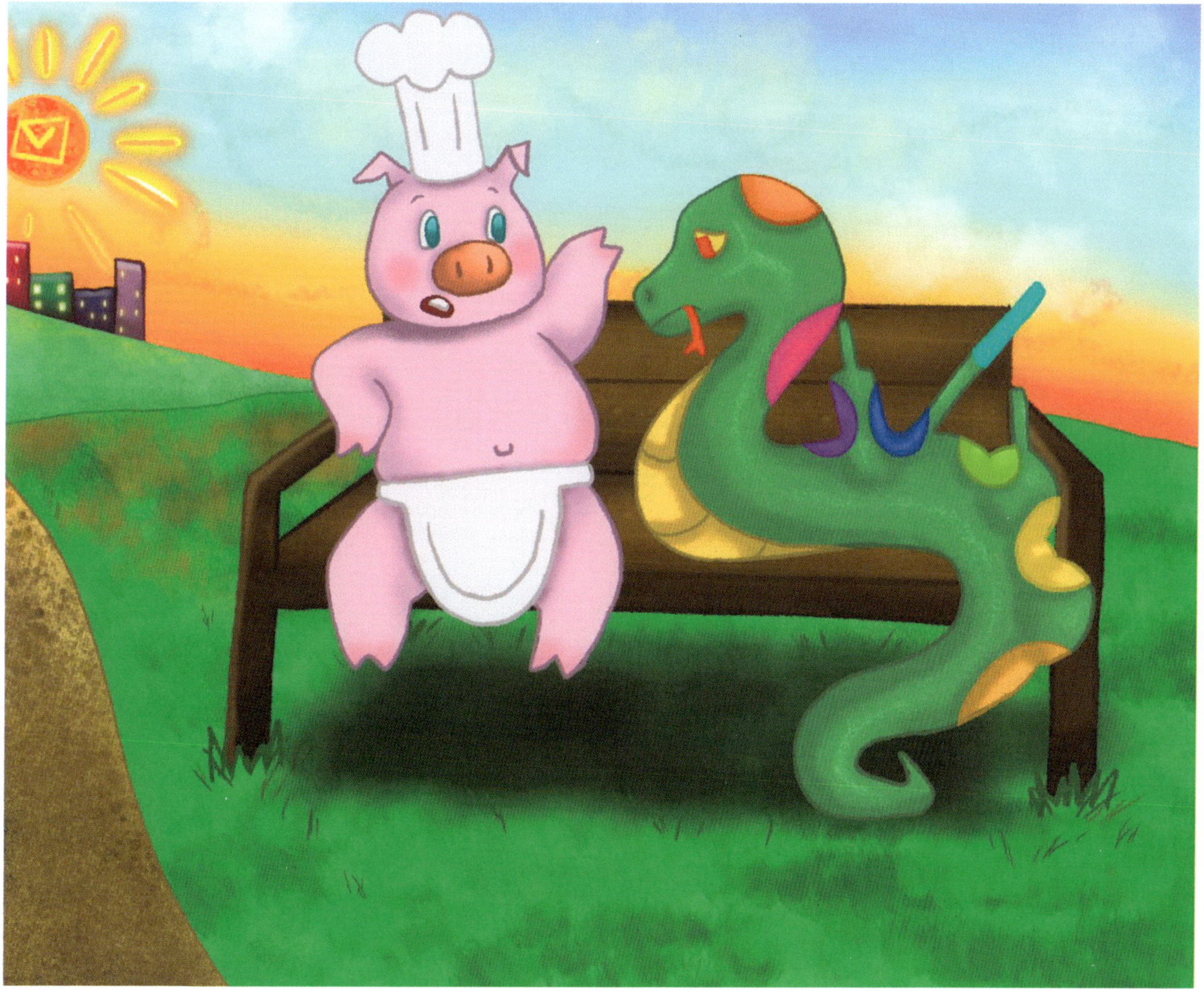

"That's because you are very hungry Kenneth" said Melvin, "I will make you something nice to eat and then you'll feel on top of the world"
"That sounds great" said Kenneth, "thank you very much"

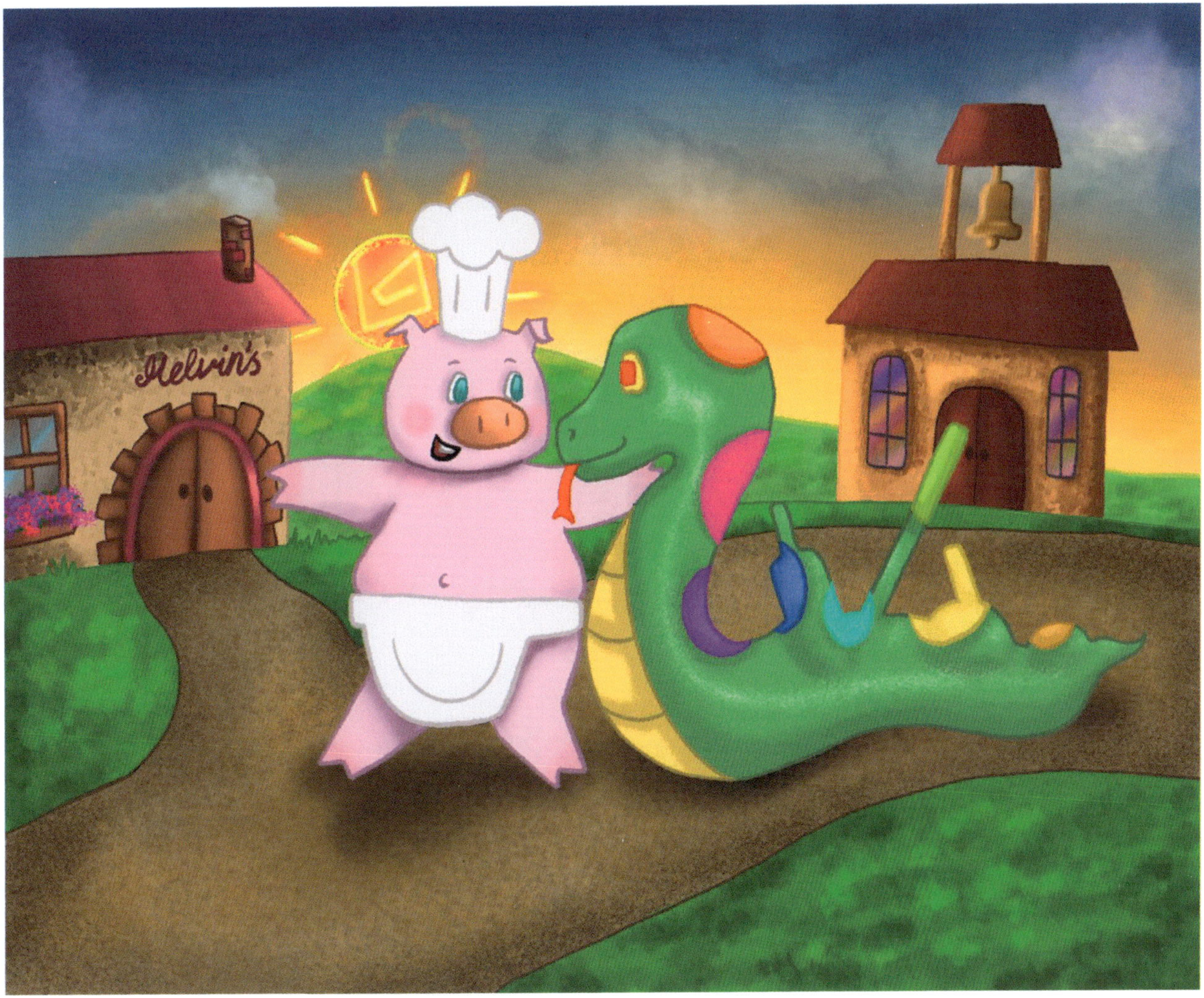
Melvin's

"Here you go" said Melvin, "I've made you a really big cake with a jelly on top"
"Oh wow" said Kenneth, "that looks lovely and the jelly is really wobbly"

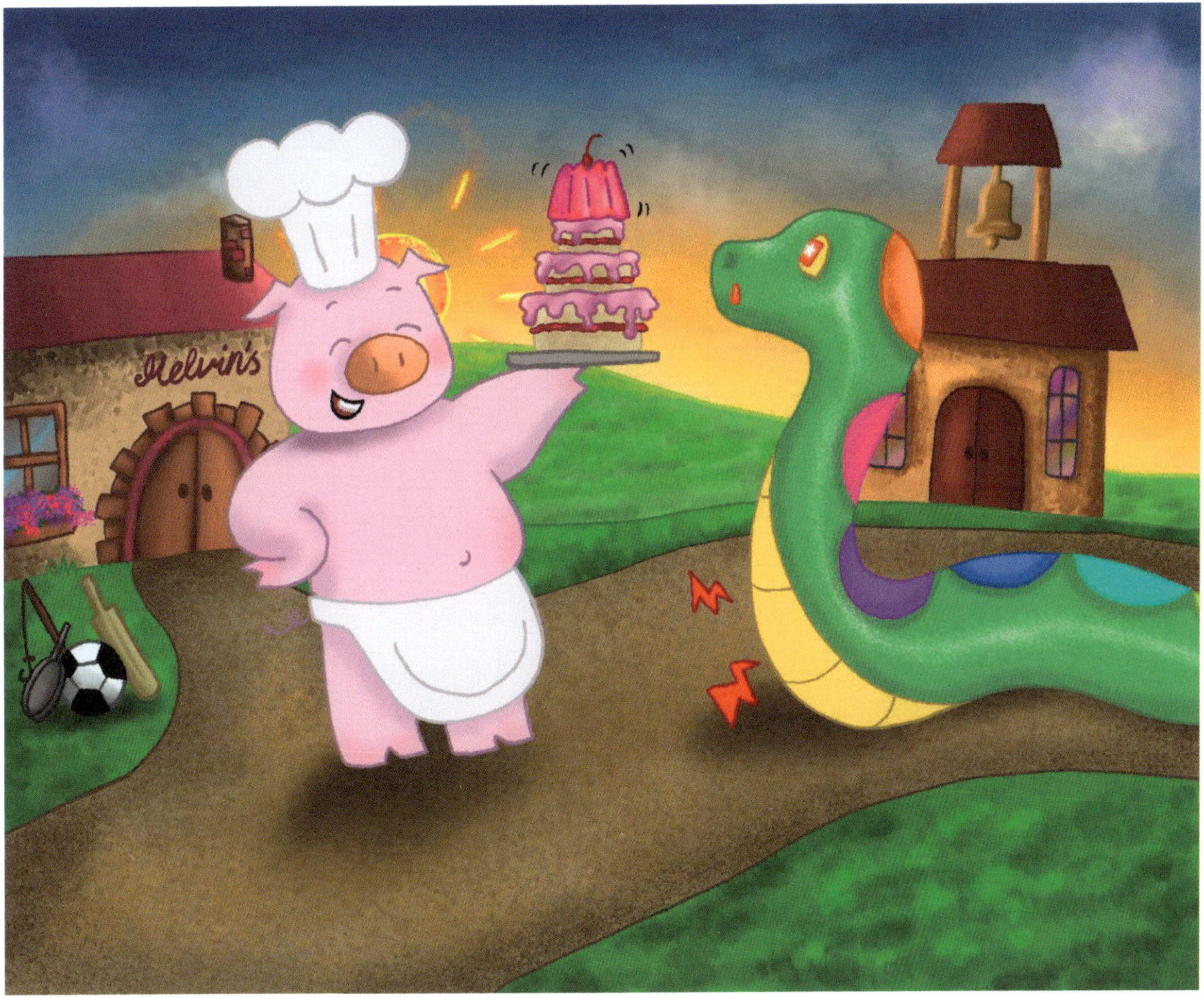
Melvin's

"That was really tasty" said Kenneth, "I am full up and feel happy inside"
"That was one of my best cakes, I'm not going to lie" said Melvin, "plus I spoke to your friends and they are happy to see you again. They want to play with you again"

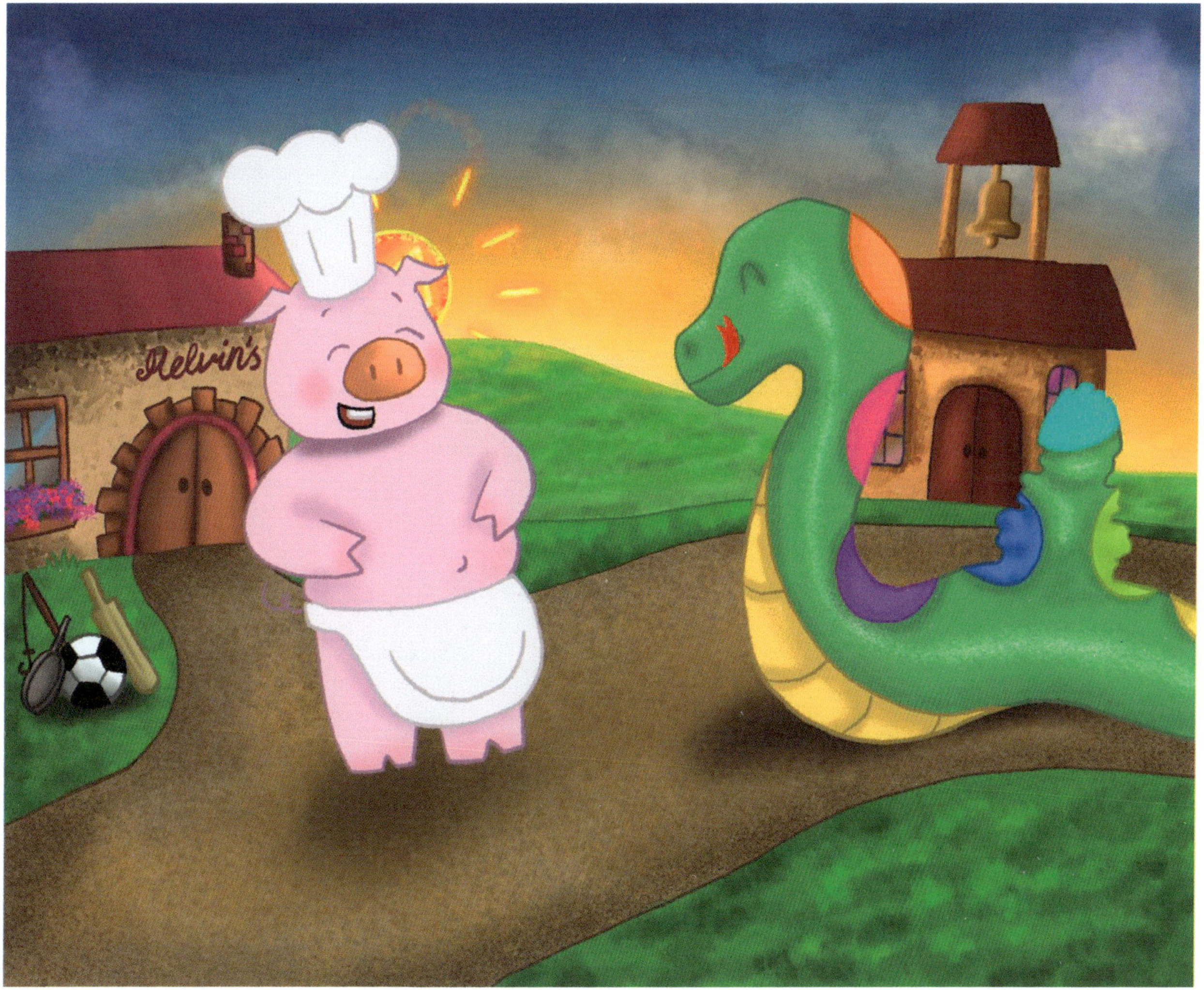
Melvin's

"I'm going to slither home and have a nap on a pillow" said Kenneth, "but then I will play will my friends and I won't eat their things anymore. CAKE!!"

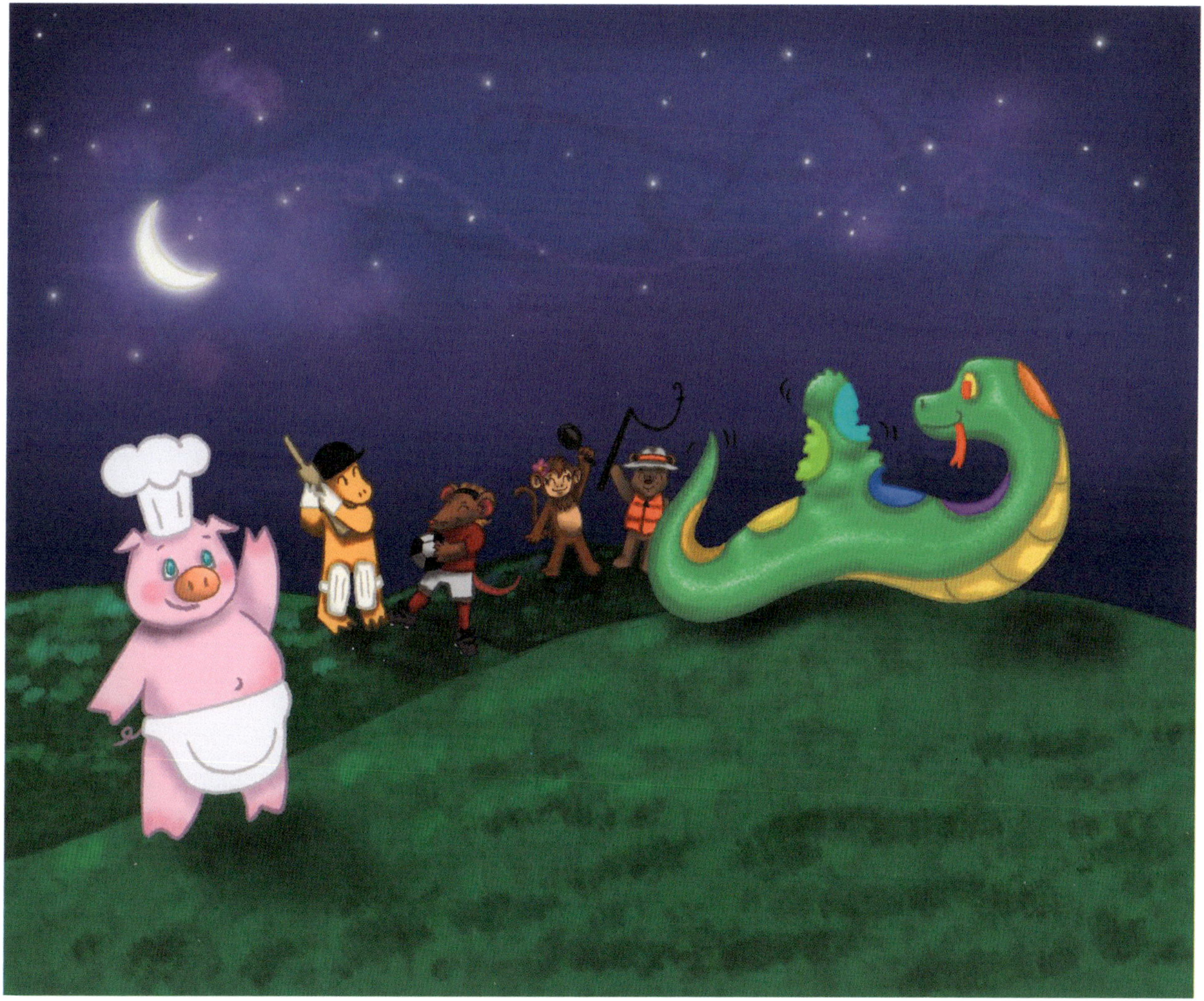

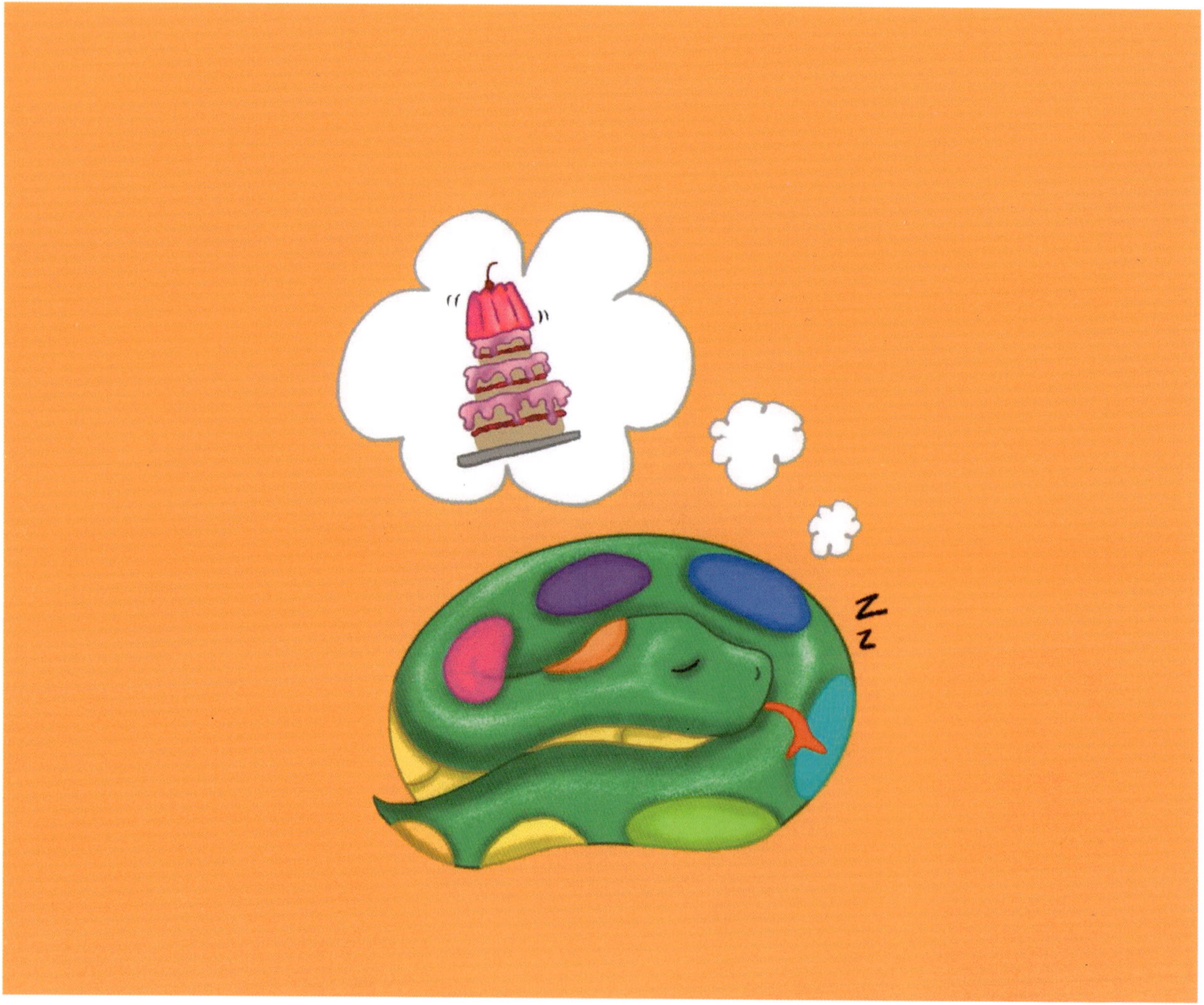

Printed in Great Britain
by Amazon